Jake and the Scrambled Snake

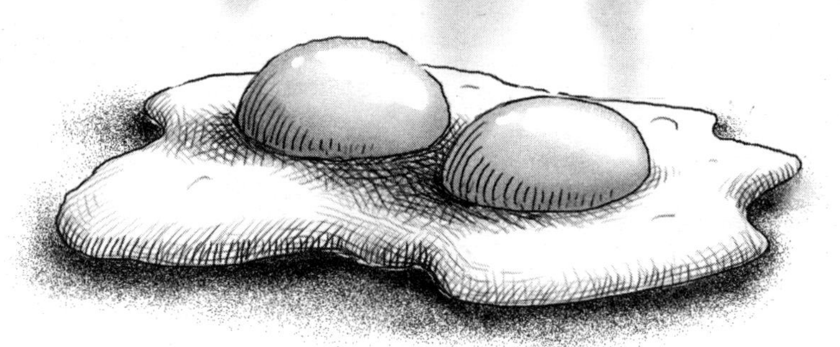

by Phil Callaway

JAKE AND THE SCRAMBLED SNAKE

Published by coolreading.com
Red Deer, Alberta, Canada
Managing Editor: Mike Kooman.

Canadian Cataloguing in Publication Data

Callaway, Phil.
Jake and the big hairy lie

ISBN 1-55305-029-0

I. Title.
PS8555.A5113J35 2001 jC813'.6 C2001-910032-9
PZ7.C1328Jasc 2001

Printed in Canada

For Stephen and Jeffrey.

Proof that brothers
can be friends, too.

Remember: Fear is like a baby.
It grows when you nurse it.

There are three things I don't like at all: poached eggs, climbing trees, and snakes. My big brother Jake loves all three. He loves climbing oak trees any time of the year and eating eggs every morning. Poached eggs. Scrambled eggs. Hard-boiled eggs. He even likes snakes. We were doing dishes together the other night and talking about these things.

"Hey," he said, sliding a plate into the soapy sink, "did you hear that a snake climbed out of Mrs. Wilson's toilet yesterday and she's moving out of town?"

"You mean the snake or Mrs. Wilson?"

He laughed. "Mrs. Wilson, of course."

"You mean the Mrs. Wilson down the road?" I asked, scrubbing disgusting caked-on yellow stuff from a plate.

"Yup," said my brother. "The snake's loose near our farm now. Little kids should stay indoors."

"I'm not a little kid," I said, still scraping at the egg. "What kind of snake is it?"

"A black mamba," said Jake. "It's from the zoo, I guess. They don't usually live around here."

"What's a black mamba?"

"It's big, it's mean, and it's fast," said my brother. "We learned about them in school. The world record is 14 feet. They show up just about anywhere. In toilets and drainpipes and sinks. They can hang from ceilings or drop from trees and they especially love chicken eggs."

I pulled my hands from the sink and squinted at the soapy suds. "Chicken eggs, huh? What are we gonna do about it?" I moved away from the sink and wiped the counter slowly, still keeping an eye on the sink.

"We're gonna watch the chicken coop, that's what we're gonna do."

"I'll give you five bucks to put your hands in the sink and finish my dishes," I said.

Jake laughed.

I stopped scrubbing the counter and stared out the

window. “Mom told me to have a bath tonight,” I said. “You don’t think a snake could get in our bathtub, do you?”

“Na,” said Jake. “But then again, you never know.”

That night just before dark we climbed the old oak tree behind our house. I was scared to death I'd fall. "Don't look down," said my brother. "You'll be fine."

The chicken coop was clearly visible through a wide opening in the branches. We were proud of that chicken coop. It seemed to shine brightly even at night. We had spent all of June building it. Crafting little doorways for the chickens. Running wire along the ground to keep out thieves. We even painted it red and white and hooked up real electricity. In August we hoped to sell eggs at the market and make our first million.

"I like the dark," said Jake.

"Why's that?"

"It's the only time I can see the stars."

"Did you know that the sun is brighter than 14 trillion fireflies?" Jake asked. I didn't know that. And I didn't know where Jake came up with these things. He was the smartest kid I'd ever met.

"I was reading about snakes at school," continued Jake, "and I learned some pretty cool stuff."

"Like what?" I asked, staring straight ahead at the setting sun.

"Well, for one thing, there aren't any snakes in Ireland, New Zealand, or Newfoundland. And rattlesnakes can't hear the sound of their own rattles."

"Black mambas don't have rattles, do they?"

"Nope," said Jake, "just big fangs."

"Do you think black mambas can climb trees?" I asked, looking down for the first time.

Jake said they could. That they sometimes looked for food in oak trees. "You're not scared, are you?" he asked.

"Well..." I shrugged, "maybe a little."

"Don't worry," Jake grinned, "they bite you and you're dead before you hit the ground. You won't feel much at all."

I hung tightly onto the branches and stared at the horizon.

When Jake finally stopped grinning he put a finger to his lips and told me to listen. The chickens were growing restless. And clucking loudly. "It's the kind of noise a chicken makes while its eggs are being stolen," Jake said.

Sure enough, it was the snake.

We watched the thief slide its slender nine-foot-long body out of the coop and pause, its ugly head swaying from side to side. The face was paler than the rest of it. Greenish-brown eyes protruded from its coffin-shaped head. Black specks were sprinkled along the back half of its greenish tail.

"Look," whispered Jake, "you can tell it's been eating eggs. Probably four or five of them. See? They're stuck in its throat."

Jake was right. The snake slithered along to a small round hole in the fence and poked its head through. But the eggs held it back. It pushed and struggled until the eggs in its throat gave way one by one: Pop. Pop. Pop.

Then the thief was gone, through the tall grass and into the night.

"There's always something to be glad about," said Jake.

"Like what?" I asked.

"Well, in the rain forest of Borneo there's a ribbon-flat paradise tree snake that glides from tree to tree like a flying squirrel."

"Do they live around here?" I asked.

"Maybe," said Jake. "There

might be one in the zoo."

"You mean the zoo the black mamba escaped from?"

"Yep."

Jake was grinning again.

We sat in the old oak tree wondering what to do next. My mind thought of a hundred solutions, but none of them made much sense. "Maybe you could shoot the snake," I said, finally.

"Our pellet gun isn't big enough," he replied. "It would just make the thing mad."

"What about poison, or a slingshot, or a trap?" I suggested.

Jake thought they might work. "Snakes are pretty smart though," he reminded me. "We've gotta out-think him."

That night I checked under my bed before crawling into it. I even checked the ceiling before turning off the light.

"If you corner a black mamba," said my brother from the bunk above mine, "it will raise its head off the ground about three feet and let out a hollow-sounding hiss. If that happens, just freeze. Don't move. They'll usually leave you alone.

But if one attacks you, go tell your mother right away.

"Snakes smell with their tongues," said Jake. "They don't have eyelids and they can't blink. That's why they just seem to stare at you when you get close."

"We better call the zoo," I said.

"I already did," said my brother.

I couldn't sleep for at least two hours after that and Jake wouldn't let me flip the light on. So I lay awake in the dark, scared and wondering what to do. I didn't want to see a bathtub ever again. Or do dishes in the sink. Or climb that old oak tree. My summer was being ruined by a stupid snake.

Just before I drifted off to sleep I prayed that God would make my brother smarter so he'd think of something.

And the next day he did.

We ate scrambled eggs for breakfast. I was trying to hide mine under some toast. “These are disgusting,” I said to no one in particular. Suddenly Jake turned to me with the widest grin I’d ever seen on his face. When I asked him what was so funny he said, “You just wait and see.”

And the grin stayed there all day.

That evening, as the sun

began to set behind the purple hills, we climbed back up the old oak tree and waited. A cricket was keeping its family awake nearby. An owl hooted softly.

"Owls always hunt at night," said Jake. "I heard they can carry little kids away in their claws."

"I'm not a little kid," I said.

Half an hour passed. My rear end was so sore I felt like I was one hundred and fifty years old. My eyelids wanted to shut too. "Maybe we should climb down," I said, yawning. "I don't want to fall asleep up here."

"Sshh," whispered Jake, holding up one hand. "The snake's getting hungry, I just know it."

Once again, Jake was right.

Moments later the chickens grew restless and the clucking grew louder. "Help! Thief!" they seemed to say. We watched the snake slither out of the coop; its ugly coffin head swaying from side to side. It didn't blink at all. I was pretty sure it could see us up in the tree.

"Look," I whispered. "More eggs...stuck in its throat."

The snake slithered along to the small hole in the fence and poked its head through. "It'll be gone again," I said to Jake. "You'd better do something." But Jake wasn't there. Then I saw him. He had climbed quietly from the tree and grabbed a shovel. Slowly he approached the coop. I hung on to a branch, almost too scared to watch.

The snake pushed and

struggled, but there was no popping sound this time. It thrashed about wildly, trying to force its bulging neck through the tiny hole. But the snake was stuck. Jake stood before it now like he'd just won the Superbowl. "It worked, it worked!" he yelled, thrusting his arms in the air. "We got him, we got him!"
Celebrating with him were two guys with snake-catching gear. They looked a lot like zookeepers.

Jake turned and looked up at me with that same old grin on his face.

"How did you do it?" I asked in amazement.

Jake didn't say anything. He just laughed until he had to sit down. "Hard-boiled eggs," he said at last. "My favorite."

I realized then that my hand hurt from holding onto the branch so tightly.

"Climb down," said my brother. "We have one more thing to do."

I climbed down.

And we laughed together all the way to Mrs. Wilson's house.

Phil is the best-selling author of seven books, and an internationally renowned speaker and storyteller. Folks call him a humorist, but his fifth grade teacher didn't find him very funny. Phil's writings have won more than a dozen awards and been translated into languages like Polish, Chinese, Spanish, German and English, which is amazing when you consider that Phil got a D- in French class. Phil writes very serious books like *I Used To Have Answers… Now I Have Kids*, and *Who Put the Skunk in the Trunk?*

He lives in Alberta, Canada with his wife Ramona and their three children, ages eleven to fourteen.

Phil likes snakes as much as bugs like windshields. He hopes this book has helped you learn to laugh when life gets scary. “I want kids to know that prayer and trust are bigger than fear,” says Phil. “Fear is the little darkroom where negatives are developed. Courage is fear that has said its prayers.”

If you want to contact Phil
or find out about his other books,
check out
www.coolreading.com/philcallaway